Ladybird Rea

Zipp and Pipp
Find a Flower

To access the audio and digital versions
of this book:

1 Go to **www.ladybirdeducation.co.uk**
2 Click "Unlock book"
3 Enter the code below

YvY6ozjhEp

Notes to teachers, parents, and carers

The *Ladybird Readers* Beginner level helps young language learners to become familiar with key conversational phrases in English. The language introduced has clear real-life applications, giving children the tools to hold their first conversations in English.

This book focuses on helping others and provides practice of saying "This is fun" and "This is not fun".

There are some activities to do in this book. They will help children practice these skills:

 Speaking Listening* Writing Reading Singing*

*To complete these activities, listen to the audio downloads available at **www.ladybirdeducation.co.uk**

Series Editor: Sorrel Pitts
Text adapted by Sorrel Pitts
Song lyrics by Fiona Davis

LADYBIRD BOOKS

UK | USA | Canada | Ireland | Australia
India | New Zealand | South Africa

Ladybird Books is part of the Penguin Random House group of companies
whose addresses can be found at global.penguinrandomhouse.com.
www.penguin.co.uk   www.puffin.co.uk   www.ladybird.co.uk

 Penguin
Random House
UK

Text adapted from *My Little Pony* episode "Portrait of a Princess" by Hasbro Inc., 2023
This version first published by Ladybird Books, 2023
001

Licensed by:

Printed in China

The authorized representative in the EEA is Penguin Random House Ireland, Morrison Chambers, 32 Nassau Street, Dublin, D02 YH68

A CIP catalogue record for this book is available from the British Library

ISBN: 978–0–241–61693–2

All correspondence to:
Ladybird Books
Penguin Random House Children's
One Embassy Gardens, 8 Viaduct Gardens, London SW11 7BW

MIX
Paper from
responsible sources
FSC® C018179

Ladybird Readers

Zipp and Pipp
Find a Flower

Based on the *My Little Pony* episode
"Portrait of a Princess"

Picture words

Zipp

Pipp

fun

phone

petals

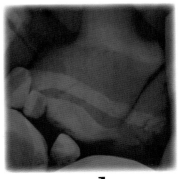

rocks

"There is a flower on this beach," says Zipp. "Can we find it?"

"This is fun," says Zipp.

Pipp is on her phone.

Then, Zipp sees petals on the beach.

8

"Look, Pipp!" Zipp says.
"Petals! We are near the flower."

"It is the flower!" says Zipp.

"I cannot send a picture to our friends," says Pipp.

"Stop taking pictures, Pipp," says Zipp.

"This is not fun."

14

"We can have fun," says Pipp.
"You are my sister."

15

"Listen!" says Zipp. "Rocks!"

"Oh no!" says Pipp.
"That is bad!"

17

"I can see the beach,"
says Zipp. "We can go!"

"The beach is fun!" say Zipp
and Pipp.

Your turn!

1 **Talk with a friend.** 💬

Can you see a flower?

Yes, I can.

Can you see a phone?

No, I cannot.

20

2 Listen and read. Match. 🎧 📖

1 Pipp is on her phone.

2 Zipp sees petals on the beach.

3 "This is not fun."

4 "We can have fun," says Pipp.

3 **Listen. Put a** ✓ **by the correct words.**

1 a "Look, Pipp!" ✓
  b "Listen, Pipp!" ☐

2 a "We are near
    the flower." ☐
  b "It is the flower!" ☐

3 a "Stop taking
    pictures." ☐
  b "I cannot send
    a picture." ☐

4 a "I can see the beach." ☐
  b "The beach is fun!" ☐

4 **Listen. Write the first letters.**

1  beach

2  petals

3  rocks

5 Sing the song. 🎵

Zipp and Pipp are at the beach.
It is a sunny day.
"This is fun! This is fun!"

Zipp finds a flower,
But Pipp is on her phone.
"This is not fun! This is not fun!"

Pipp stops taking pictures
And the sisters play.
"We can have fun! We can have fun!"

"Oh no! Listen to the rocks!"
Then Zipp and Pipp go.
"The beach is fun! The beach is fun!"